ALFIE

Alfie and Grandma

Shirley Hughes

Red Fox

Looking for Winnie

Alfie's grandma lived in the country with her
two cats, Juno and Belle. The cats slept in baskets
in the kitchen, near the stove because they liked
being warm. Just up the lane from Grandma's
house lived Jim and Lorna Gatting. Their son
was grown up and had gone to live far away
in New Zealand. They had a dog called
Shep and a pig and some hens and two
pet tortoises, Winnie and Fred, who
were very old. Fred was eighty-nine
and nobody knew how old
Winnie was; perhaps nearly
a hundred, Lorna said.

In winter Winnie and Fred were sleepy and liked to be indoors in their cosy boxes full of straw. In summertime they lived outside in the Gattings' back garden. They had a pen with a little wooden house in it and a grassy space with wire around it to stop them getting out. Alfie and Annie Rose often helped to feed Winnie and Fred. They ate bits of lettuce and tomato and they specially liked wild flowers called buttercups.

Alfie often collected a big bunch of them after Jim had cut the grass. He liked watching Winnie and Fred stretch out their leathery necks to nip off the flowers and slowly chew them up in their wide tortoise jaws.

One morning when Alfie and Annie Rose and Grandma went to visit the tortoises, they found Lorna very upset. She told them that when she went out that morning, Fred was there in the pen as usual but Winnie was nowhere to be seen! She was not inside the little house. Lorna had searched in the long grass around the pen but there was no Winnie!

"She must have got out somehow," said Lorna anxiously. "She always was a bit of a wanderer. But she can't have gone far because tortoises are very slow walkers."

Alfie and Grandma and Annie Rose helped Lorna to search for Winnie. They looked all over the garden, under the bushes and around the shed.

You can't call or whistle for a tortoise like you can for a cat or dog. Anyway, Alfie had a feeling that Winnie would not have taken any notice even if she *had* heard them calling her.

At supper time Alfie was too worried about Winnie to eat much.

"Perhaps she fell into the pond," he said.
"Can Winnie swim?" he asked Grandma.

Grandma was doubtful. "I hope she didn't get into the lane," she said. "I don't like to think of her lying on her back in a ditch. Once tortoises are on their backs they can't get the right way up again."

At bed time it was still light and sunny. Grandma said that Alfie and Annie Rose could come with her for one last Winnie hunt.

They set out up the road, looking carefully in the ditch all the way. They walked past the Gattings' house and turned into the lane where old Mrs Hall lived. Still there was no sign of Winnie. Then Grandma said that they really would have to turn back. "Winnie couldn't possibly have got this far anyway," she said.

Mrs Hall's cottage was very neat and tidy, with neat, tidy flowerbeds in her garden. Leading up to the front gate was a neat and tidy path picked out with big round stones on either side, which were painted white.

"Come on, Alfie, it's long past your bed time," said Grandma.

But Alfie hung back. He was looking very hard at Mrs Hall's stones. He noticed that one of them was not white but brown. He ran over to get a closer look, and then he saw that it was not a stone at all, it was Winnie!

"Well spotted, Alfie!" said Grandma, giving him a hug. "I never imagined that Winnie could walk so far. Tortoises can't be such slow walkers after all."

Alfie picked up Winnie and carried her carefully back to the Gattings' house. Lorna was delighted. She just could not stop saying how clever Alfie was to have found her, and how naughty it was of Winnie to go off like that and pretend to be a stone.

They carried Winnie into the garden and put her back in the pen.
She stretched out her neck and looked about with her beady black tortoise
eyes. Alfie and Annie Rose fed her with an extra supply of buttercups.

"I'm *so* glad we've got her back," said Grandma.

But Fred did not seem particularly pleased
to see Winnie. He just went inside his shell
and would not come out.

A Journey to the North Pole

Alfie and Annie Rose and Mum were on a visit to Grandma's house. Outside it was cold and wet. Mum was upstairs doing some work on her computer. Alfie and Annie Rose were downstairs in the kitchen with Grandma.

Alfie looked out of the window. It was all steamed up. He could hardly see the garden outside. Raindrops trickled endlessly down the pane. He wrote an "A" for Alfie on it with his finger.

Then he got down on the floor
and started to build a Space Station.
But Annie Rose kept trying to join in.

"Annie Rose keeps annoying and
annoying and annoying me!" wailed
Alfie at last. "She won't play with
her own toys, she always wants to
play with mine!"

"Go away, Annie Rose!" he
told her sternly. Then Annie
Rose began to cry.

Grandma put down her potato
peeler. "Let's go for a walk," she
said.

So Alfie and Annie Rose
and Grandma struggled
into their boots and hats
and waterproofs and
went out into the rain.

The lane outside Grandma's gate had a stream running down the middle of it and plenty of mud. They held hands and slithered along together.

It was fun at first, sloshing about. But soon Annie Rose's boots were full of water.

Then she sat down in a puddle and got wet all over. Alfie's feet were rather damp too. They turned back towards home.

"What shall we do now, I wonder?" said Grandma when they were all dry again. "It's not lunchtime yet. I think we had better go on an indoor expedition." Alfie wanted to know what an expedition was and Grandma told him it was a long journey into unexplored territory.

"We'll need supplies," she said. She packed their little backpacks with some crisps and bits of apple and four biscuits, and they set out.

They went through the house pretending that each room they visited was a different country.

They went through jungles, where tigers prowled.

They swam in billowing oceans . . .

and crawled through dense undergrowth . . .

. . . and made boats to
cross fast-flowing rivers.

They climbed up steep mountain
paths beside rushing waterfalls, hanging
on to the rocky sides in case they fell in.

And when they reached the top they
pitched a tent and ate their supplies.

At last they came to the steep little wooden stairs which led up to Grandma's attic. This was the highest point in the world.

"This is the North Pole all right," said Grandma, shivering. It certainly was cold. They could hear the rain beating down on the roof. But there were so many interesting things there that Alfie and Annie Rose quite forgot they were at the North Pole.

They spent a long time exploring in old suitcases and cardboard cartons full of things which had been dumped down and forgotten.

Annie Rose found some picture postcards and a box with ribbons and bits of jewellery in it, and a handbag and a big hat. Alfie found a broken anglepoise lamp and a set of dominoes and a kite.

"Time to go back to Base Camp," said Grandma. "Let's take our treasure with us before we freeze to death."

Grandma helped them take it all down to the kitchen. It was *excellent* treasure. It lasted Alfie and Annie Rose for the rest of the day until teatime, when the sun came out.

Lost Sheep

Grandma's house had a long garden at the back and a small garden in front with a gate which led into the lane. If you walked one way you came to the road and more houses. If you walked the other way, up the hill, there were trees, hedges and fields. In the fields lived cows and sheep.

The cows went up to the farm twice a day to be milked. They walked follow-my-leader in a long straggly line. The rest of the time they stayed in the field, munching. Alfie liked the slow way they lowered their necks and pulled up great mouthfuls of grass. When he and Grandma passed by, the cows came to the fence and stood in a row, looking over curiously with big brown eyes, swishing their tails and breathing hard through their noses.

Cows were very nice. But best of all Alfie liked sheep. Sheep were his favourite animals. He especially liked the ones with black faces and bony black legs sticking out below their large woolly bodies.

The field where the sheep lived was further up the hill. When Alfie climbed the gate to say hello to them they trotted away and stood baa-ing at him from a safe distance.

One day, when Alfie and Grandma were out for a walk together, they saw a black-faced sheep standing in the middle of the lane all by herself. She was baa-ing very loudly at the other sheep and they were baa-ing back from behind the fence.

"Oh dear, that sheep's got out somehow," said Grandma. "She must have got through a hole in the fence."

"I think she wants to get back to the others," said Alfie.

As they came nearer to the sheep, she ran on up the lane. Every so often she stopped and looked through the fence as though she was trying to find a way back. But when Alfie and Grandma came close to try to help her, she shook her woolly tail at them and ran on. She wouldn't let them catch up with her.

The more they hurried behind her, the faster she ran. Soon she had left her own field behind and reached another field full of cows. They put their heads over the fence and moo-ed at her. The poor sheep baa-ed back. She looked very puzzled and lost.

Then she ran on again. She ran to the top of the hill where big trees grew on either side of the lane.

"We'd better not follow her any further," said Grandma. "She'll just run on and on and we'll never be able to catch her."

Alfie and Grandma stood still and wondered what to do. The sheep stopped too. She stood a good distance away, but she turned her head to look at them and baa-ed anxiously.

"Let's just stand here for a while and see what happens," said Grandma.

Alfie and Grandma stood together hand in hand on the grassy bank. Alfie found it very hard to stand still for long but he pretended he was a tree growing by the fence and that made it easier.

For a long while the sheep just stood and stared at them. Then she started to trot back down the lane towards them. Grandma and Alfie squeezed each other's hands tightly. They stood as still as still. The sheep came nearer and paused. Then she stepped daintily past them, holding up her head proudly and pretending not to notice them at all.

Alfie and Grandma stood and watched her large woolly back hurrying
away round the bend in the lane. They waited a while before they started
to walk home. When they reached the field where the sheep lived the lane
was empty.

"Our sheep must have found her own way back into the field with the
others," said Grandma.

Alfie climbed the gate to look. The sheep turned their heads to look back at him. It was very hard to tell which was the one who had got lost.

"Well done, black-faced sheep!" shouted Alfie, waving. And all the sheep baa-ed back.

Grandma's House

Alfie's grandma lives in the country. This is a picture-map of all the places around where she lives. Can you find where Winnie walked to? What about the lane where Alfie and Grandma found the sheep? What a lot of adventures they have!

Stream where Alfie and Mum went exploring

Woods

Big rocks

Secret place where Alfie and Mum once saw a snake

Mrs Hall's cottage

Field where Alfie and Dad camped out

Jim Gatting's pig

Field where the sheep live

Grandma's pond

Grandma's house

Field where the cows live

To the main road

Jim and Lorna Gatting's house

Winnie and Fred's pen

Apple orchard

Other titles in the Alfie series:

Alfie Gets in First

Alfie's Feet

Alfie Gives a Hand

An Evening at Alfie's

Alfie and the Birthday Surprise

Alfie Wins a Prize

Alfie and the Big Boys

All About Alfie

Alfie's Weather

Alfie's Numbers

Alfie's Alphabet

Alfie's World

Annie Rose Is My Little Sister

Rhymes for Annie Rose

The Big Alfie and Annie Rose Storybook

The Big Alfie Out of Doors Storybook

ALFIE AND GRANDMA
A RED FOX BOOK 978 1 782 95515 3

Published in Great Britain by Red Fox, 2015
an imprint of Random House Children's Publishers UK
A Penguin Random House Company

Penguin
Random House
UK

1 3 5 7 9 10 8 6 4 2

Copyright © Shirley Hughes, 1992, 2001, 2006, 2015

LOOKING FOR WINNIE and GRANDMA'S HOUSE first published in *Alfie's World* © Shirley Hughes, 2006
A JOURNEY TO THE NORTH POLE first published in *Alfie Weather* © Shirley Hughes, 2001
LOST SHEEP first published in *The Big Alfie Out of Doors Storybook* © Shirley Hughes, 1992
All first published in Great Britain by The Bodley Head.

The right of Shirley Hughes to be identified as the author of this work has been asserted in accordance with the Copyright, Designs and Patents Act 1988.

Penguin Random House is committed to a sustainable future for our business, our readers and our planet. This book is made from Forest Stewardship Council® certified paper.

MIX
Paper from
responsible sources
FSC® C013123

Red Fox Books are published by Random House Children's Publishers UK,
61–63 Uxbridge Road, London W5 5SA

www.randomhousechildrens.co.uk
www.randomhouse.co.uk

Addresses for companies within The Random House Group Limited can be found at: www.randomhouse.co.uk/offices.htm

THE RANDOM HOUSE GROUP Limited Reg. No. 954009

A CIP catalogue record for this book is available from the British Library.

Printed and bound in Italy by Graphicom